Tiger Forgives

written by Dr. Mary Manz Simon
illustrated by Linda Clearwater

© 2003 Mary Manz Simon. © 2003 Standard Publishing, Cincinnati, Ohio. A division of Standex International Corporation. All rights reserved. Sprout logo is a trademark of Standard Publishing. First Virtues™ is a trademark of Standard Publishing. Printed in Italy. Project editor: Jennifer Holder. Design: Robert Glover and Suzanne Jacobson. Scripture quoted from the *HOLY BIBLE, Contemporary English Version.* Copyright © 1995 by American Bible Society. Used by permission. ISBN 0-7847-1413-4

09 08 07 06 05 04 03   9 8 7 6 5 4 3 2 1

Standard Publishing

cincinnati, ohio

www.standardpub.com

Tiger, Tiger,
share today,
what the Bible
has to say...

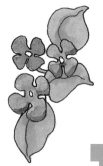

To forgive means
move on past.
Don't let angry
feelings last.

If a friend
steps on my toe,
I will pardon her,
you know.

When someone won't share a toy, I forgive that girl or boy.

Then we have
a brand new start.
I feel kindness
in my heart.

"**I** forgive"
are words I say
almost every
single day.

If a friend
does not play fair,
I forgive
to show I care.

God forgives,
so I can, too.
That is what
I try to do.

"**I** forgive"
God says to you.
Are those words
that you say, too?

"Forgive others,
and God will forgive you."
Luke 6:37